Quentin Blake

ZAGAZOO

RED
FOX

for Tom

A Red Fox Book

Published by Random House Children's Books
20 Vauxhall Bridge Road, London SW1V 2SA

A division of The Random House Group Ltd
London Melbourne Sydney Auckland
Johannesburg and agencies throughout the world

1 3 5 7 9 10 8 6 4 2

First published in Great Britain by
Jonathan Cape Limited, 1998
Red Fox edition 2000

Printed in Singapore by Tien Wah Press (PTE) Ltd

THE RANDOM HOUSE GROUP Limited Reg. No. 954009

www.randomhouse.co.uk

ISBN 0 09 926534 6

Once upon a time there was a happy couple.
Their names were George and Bella.

They spent their days…

…making model aeroplanes…

…dusting…

…and eating strawberry
and vanilla ice-cream.

One day the postman brought
them a strange-looking parcel.

They unwrapped it together.

Inside there was a little pink creature, as pretty as could be. On it was a label which said:

Its name is Zagazoo.

How lovely it was. George and Bella spent happy days throwing it from one to another.

Zagazoo was not *quite* perfect.

But his happy smile
seemed to make
up for that...

...and George and Bella went
on happily throwing him to each other,
higher and higher.
It was a wonderful life.

AND THEN ONE DAY...

…George and Bella got up in the morning and discovered that Zagazoo had changed into a huge baby vulture.

Its screeches were terrifying.

They were even worse at night.

"What shall we do?" said George.
"How can we stand it?"

But then...

…they got up one morning and discovered that Zagazoo had changed into a small elephant.

He knocked over the furniture.

He pulled the tablecloth off the table.

He ate anything he could lay his trunk on.

"This is appalling," said Bella.
"How can we cope?"

But then…

… one morning they got up
and discovered that Zagazoo had
changed into a warthog.

He rolled about in anything that looked like mud and ran about the house with it. "This is dreadful," said George. "There's just no end to it."

But then…

…they got up one morning and discovered that Zagazoo had changed into a small bad-tempered dragon.

He scorched the carpet.

He set light to the cardigan of an old lady who had come to sell raffle-tickets.

“This is terrible,” said Bella. “In no time he’s going to burn the house down.”

But then...

...they got up one morning and discovered that Zagazoo had changed into a bat that hung on to the curtains and wailed.

And then the next day he was the warthog again.

And then some days he was the elephant…

…and some days he was the bad-tempered dragon.

"This is driving us to distraction," said Bella. "If only he'd stay as one thing."

But then…

…one morning they got up and Zagazoo had changed into a strange hairy creature.

"Oh no!" said Bella. "I preferred the elephant."
"Or even the warthog," said George.

Every day the creature went on getting bigger… and hairier… and stranger.

"Suppose it never stops," said Bella.

"It doesn't bear thinking about," said George.
"It's turning my hair grey already.

What will become of us?"

BUT THEN…

… one morning George and Bella got up and discovered that Zagazoo had changed into a young man with perfect manners.

"Let me get you a chair, Mama," he said.

"And let me get you both some breakfast."

"And if there are any odd jobs that need doing, just let me know."

Zagazoo soon made friends with a young woman called Mirabelle.

They found they were both interested in motorcycle maintenance ...

...flower arrangement...

...and eating fruit salad.

It was not long before
they knew that they wanted
to spend the rest of
their lives together.

But when they went to tell George
and Bella, they discovered that they had
changed into a pair of large brown pelicans.

You could tell they were pleased at the news
by the way they clattered their beaks.

Isn't life amazing!